W9-AWQ-261

**OFFICIALLY NOTED**

11/19 Moisture damage on top. yu

Konrad Richter

# Wipe your feet, Santa Claus!

*Pictures by Józef Wilkoń*

*Translated by Rosemary Lanning*

North-South Books
New York   London   Toronto

The kitchen door flew open and Stephen came rushing indoors.

"Hey, listen!" he cried, excitedly. "Guess what I've been doing...?"

"I know what you *haven't* done," snapped his mother, "and that's take your boots off. Look at the mess you're making on my nice clean floor! How often do I have to tell you not to come into the house with dirty boots on?"

"I'm sorry," mumbled Stephen. Glumly he turned round and crept outside again. Now he didn't feel like telling his mother how much fun he'd had in the forest, feeding all the animals.

Slowly he walked across the
yard toward the barn. He decided to
help his uncle to load the sled with
hay for tomorrow.

Uncle John had almost finished his work in the barn.

"Hello Stephen. Why are you looking so miserable?" he asked. "Aren't you excited? Santa Claus is coming tonight!"

Stephen went pale. He was so surprised that he couldn't answer. He'd forgotten all about Santa Claus. Today of all days he had to get into trouble over his boots.

But he stamped his foot defiantly and yelled, "Santa Claus is silly. I don't like nuts or tangerines and he can keep his stupid presents!"

Stephen ran back to the house, sat down on the steps and stared into space. Would Santa Claus know that he always came into the house without wiping his feet? And could Santa Claus have heard what Stephen had just said about him in the barn? Perhaps he wouldn't bring him any presents now!

He hadn't been sitting there long when he heard his mother calling. "Come indoors, Stephen. Santa Claus will be here soon!"

Stephen's mother was just lighting a candle when they heard a heavy knock on the door. In came Santa Claus, a big man with an enormous red coat and a long white beard. As he walked slowly into the room, Stephen crept away into the far corner, and hid under the table.

Now he could see nothing but
Santa Claus's big black boots
through the table legs.

But what was that he saw? Small lumps of snow were falling off Santa Claus's boots onto the floor, where they melted.

When Stephen saw this, he jumped up and cried: "Look, Santa Claus has dirty boots, too!"

Santa Claus and Stephen's mother stared in silence at the dirty boots. Then Santa Claus began to laugh out loud. Stephen's mother just had to laugh, too.

Finally Santa Claus sat
down, patted Stephen on the
back and said, "Yes, my dear
Stephen, even Santa Claus makes
mistakes sometimes. Now we'd
both better promise your mother
that we won't run around with
dirty shoes again."

Pleased at the way things had turned out, Stephen nodded and made his promise. He began to think Santa Claus wasn't so bad after all. "He's quite nice, really," he said to himself.

That night, when Stephen went to bed, he found a plate of tangerines, candy, nuts and two small presents on his bedside table. And he silently renewed his promise not to walk around the house with dirty shoes ever again.

When he fell asleep he had lovely dreams about all the animals in the forest.

Copyright © 1985 Nord-Süd Verlag, Mönchaltorf, Switzerland
*First published in Switzerland under the title* Sankt Nikolaus kommt
English text copyright © 1985 Abelard-Schuman Ltd
Copyright English language edition under the imprint
North-South Books © 1985 Rada Matija AG, Staefa, Switzerland

First published in the United States, Great Britain and Canada
in 1985 by North-South Books, an imprint of Rada Matija AG.

Reprinted in 1986.

Distributed in the United States by
Henry Holt and Company, Inc., 521 Fifth Avenue,
New York, New York 10175.

Library of Congress Cataloging in Publication Data

Richter, Konrad.
  Wipe your feet, Santa Claus!

  Translation of: Sankt Nikolaus kommt.
  Summary: Stephen fears that his habit of coming into
the house with dirty boots will get him into trouble on
the night of santa's visit.
  I. Children's stories, German – Swiss Authors.
  [I. Santa Claus – Fiction. 2. Christmas – Fiction.
3. Boots – Fiction] I. Wilkoń, Józef, ill.    II. Title.
PZ7.R4154Wi    1985    [E]    85-7246

ISBN 0-8050-0171-9

Distributed in Great Britain by
Blackie and Son Ltd, 7 Leicester Place,
London WC2H 7BP.
British Library Cataloguing in Publication Data

Richter, Konrad
  Wipe your feet, Santa Claus!
  I. Title    II. Sankt Nikolaus kommt. *English*
III. Wilkon, Josef
  833'.914[J]    ˙ PZ7

ISBN 0-200-72870-9

Distributed in Canada by
Douglas & McIntyre Ltd., Toronto.
Canadian Cataloguing in Publication Data available in
Marc Record from National Library of Canada.
ISBN 0 88894 755 0

*Printed in Germany*